MOTHER, MOTHER, I WANT ANOTHER

by Maria Polushkin Robbins

illustrated by Jon Goodell

Alfred A. Knopf New York

o Ken

—M.P.R.

Great thanks to Trish for opening the door
to the land of book illustration

—J.G.

THIS IS A BORZOI BOOK PUBLISHED BY ALFRED A. KNOPF

Text copyright © 1978 by Maria Polushkin Robbins
Illustrations copyright © 2005 by Jon Goodell

All rights reserved under International and Pan-American Copyright Conventions. Published
in the United States by Alfred A. Knopf, an imprint of Random House Children's Books,
a division of Random House, Inc., New York, and simultaneously in Canada by Random
House of Canada Limited, Toronto. Distributed by Random House, Inc., New York.
Originally published with different illustrations by Crown Publishers in 1978.

KNOPF, BORZOI BOOKS, and the colophon are registered trademarks of Random House, Inc.

www.randomhouse.com/kids

Library of Congress Cataloging-in-Publication Data
Robbins, Maria Polushkin.
Mother, Mother, I want another / by Maria Polushkin Robbins ; illustrated by Jon Goodell.
p.   cm.
SUMMARY: In this newly illustrated edition, Mrs. Mouse is anxious to get her son to sleep
and goes off to find what she thinks he wants.
ISBN 0-375-82588-6 (trade) — ISBN 0-375-92588-0 (lib. bdg.)
[1. Mice—Fiction. 2. Sleep—Fiction. 3. Bedtime—Fiction.] I. Goodell, Jon, ill. II. Title.
PZ7.R53275Mo 2005
[E]—dc22
2004003124

MANUFACTURED IN CHINA
March 2005
10 9 8 7 6 5 4 3 2

It was bedtime in the mouse house.
Mrs. Mouse took baby mouse to his room.

She helped him
put on his pajamas
and told him
to brush his teeth.

She tucked him
into his bed
and read him
a bedtime story.

She gave him a bedtime kiss,
and then she said, "Good night."

But as she was leaving,
baby mouse started to cry.
"Why are you crying?" asked Mrs. Mouse.

"I want another, Mother."

"Another mother!" cried Mrs. Mouse.
"Where will I find another mother for my baby?"

Mrs. Mouse ran to get Mrs. Duck.

"Please, Mrs. Duck, come to our house and help put
baby mouse to bed. Tonight he wants another mother."

Mrs. Duck came and sang a song:

Quack, quack, mousie,
Don't you fret.
I'll bring you worms
Both fat and wet.

But baby mouse said,
"Mother, Mother, I want another."

Mrs. Duck went to get Mrs. Frog.

Mrs. Frog came and sang:

Croak, croak, mousie,
Close your eyes.
I will bring you
Big fat flies.

But baby mouse said,
"Mother, Mother, I want another."

Mrs. Frog went to get Mrs. Pig.

Mrs. Pig came and sang a song:

Oink, oink, mousie,
Go to sleep.
I'll bring some carrots
For you to keep.

But baby mouse said,
"Mother, Mother, I want another."

Mrs. Pig went to get Mrs. Donkey.

Mrs. Donkey came and sang a song:

Hee-haw, mousie,
Hush-a-bye.
I'll sing for you
A lullaby.

But baby mouse
had had enough.

"NO MORE MOTHERS!"
he shouted.

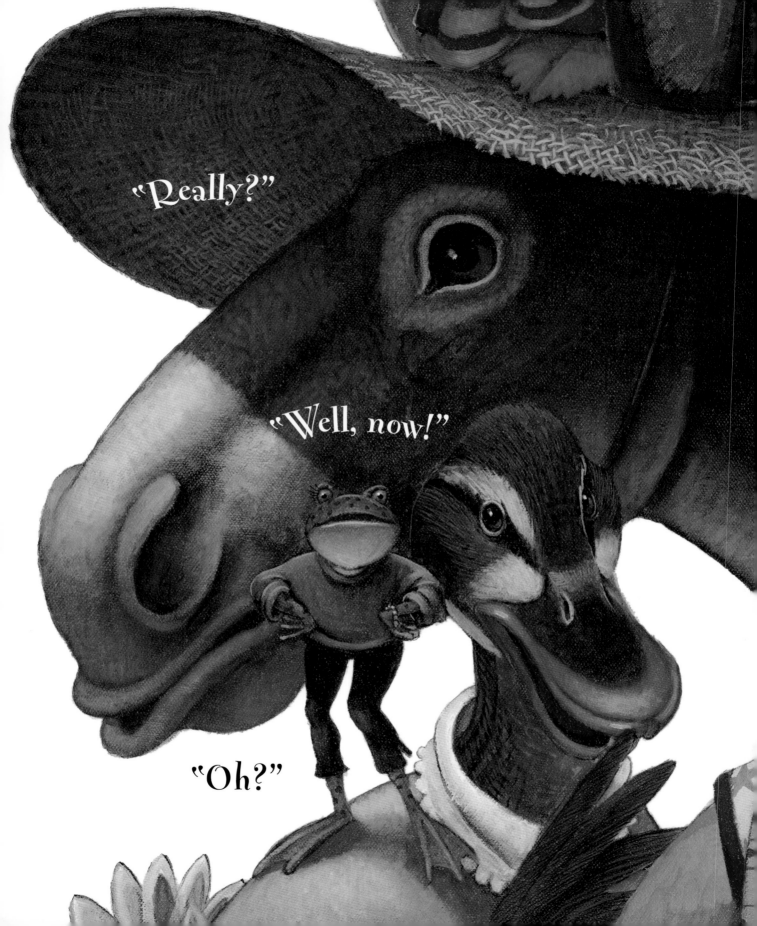

Mrs. Duck
kissed baby mouse.

Mrs. Frog kissed
baby mouse.

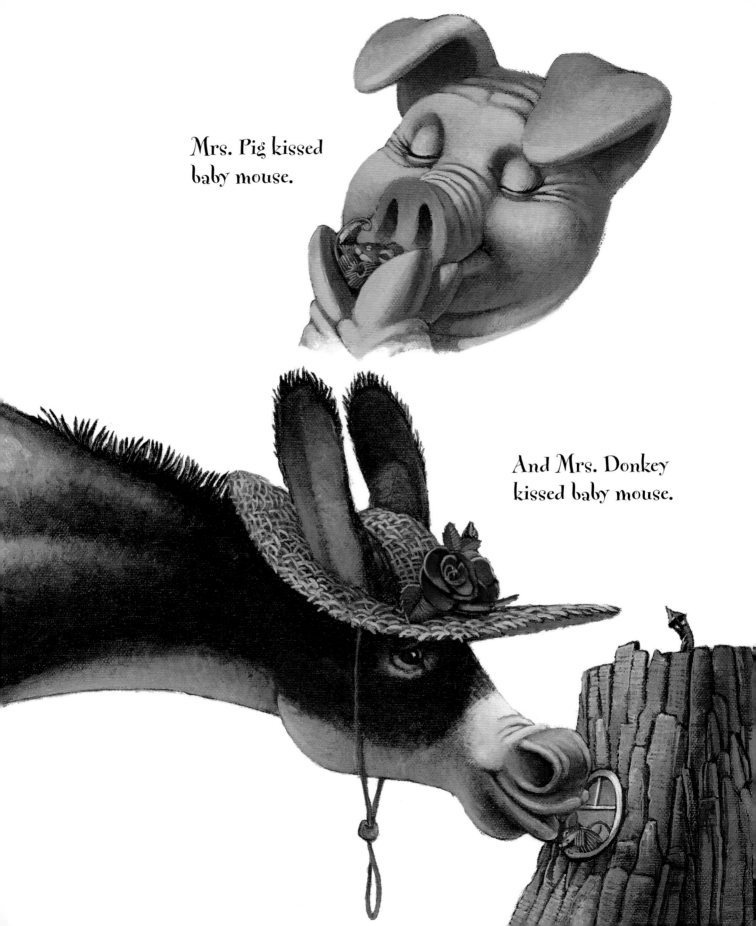

Mrs. Pig kissed
baby mouse.

And Mrs. Donkey
kissed baby mouse.

Then Mrs. Mouse gave baby mouse a drink
of water. She tucked in his blanket.

And she gave him a kiss.

Baby mouse smiled.
"May I have another, Mother?"

"Of course," said Mrs. Mouse,
and she leaned over and gave him *another* kiss.